Hello, Clifford!

by Wiley Blevins

Illustrated by Josie Yee

SCHOLASTIC INC.
New York Toronto London Auckland Sydney
Mexico City New Delhi Hong Kong Buenos Aires

I am Clifford.

I am Emily Elizabeth.

K-9
K-9
K-9
K-9
K-9
K-9
K-9
K-9

I am  Cleo.

I am  T-Bone.

"Hello, Clifford!"

"Hello!"

“Hello, T-Bone!”

“Hello!”

We are friends!

What is your name?